The
THORNBUSH

The THORNBUSH

MICHAEL LAUGHLIN

ILLUSTRATED BY
RICHARD STERGULZ

Tommy
NELSON

Thomas Nelson, Inc.
Nashville

Text © 2000 by Michael Laughlin.
Illustrations © 2000 by Richard Stergulz.

Published in Nashville, Tennessee, by Tommy Nelson™, a division of Thomas Nelson, Inc.

Library of Congress Cataloging-in-Publication Data
Laughlin, Michael, 1956-
    The thornbush / Michael Laughlin; illustrated by Richard Stergulz.
        p. cm.
    Summary: A ragged little thornbush observes the events leading up to the
crucifixion and resurrection of Jesus.
    ISBN 0-8499-5968-3
    1. Jesus Christ—Crucifixion Juvenile fiction. 2. Jesus Christ—Resurrection Juvenile
fiction. [1. Jesus Christ—Crucifixion Fiction. 2. Jesus Christ—Resurrection Fiction.]
I. Stergulz, Richard, ill. II. Title.
PZ7.L3705Th 1999
[E]—dc21

                                                                99-37002
                                                                CIP

Printed in the United States of America
00 01 02 03 WCV 9 8 7 6 5 4 3 2 1

To Emily, Chris, and Cathy,

for their prayers, support,

and encouragement,

and to Christ, our Lord,

for His guidance and inspiration.

The thornbush stared up at the moonlit sky, waiting for the warmth of the dawn. Its tiny flowers huddled together against the cold. Finally the little bush drifted off to sleep.

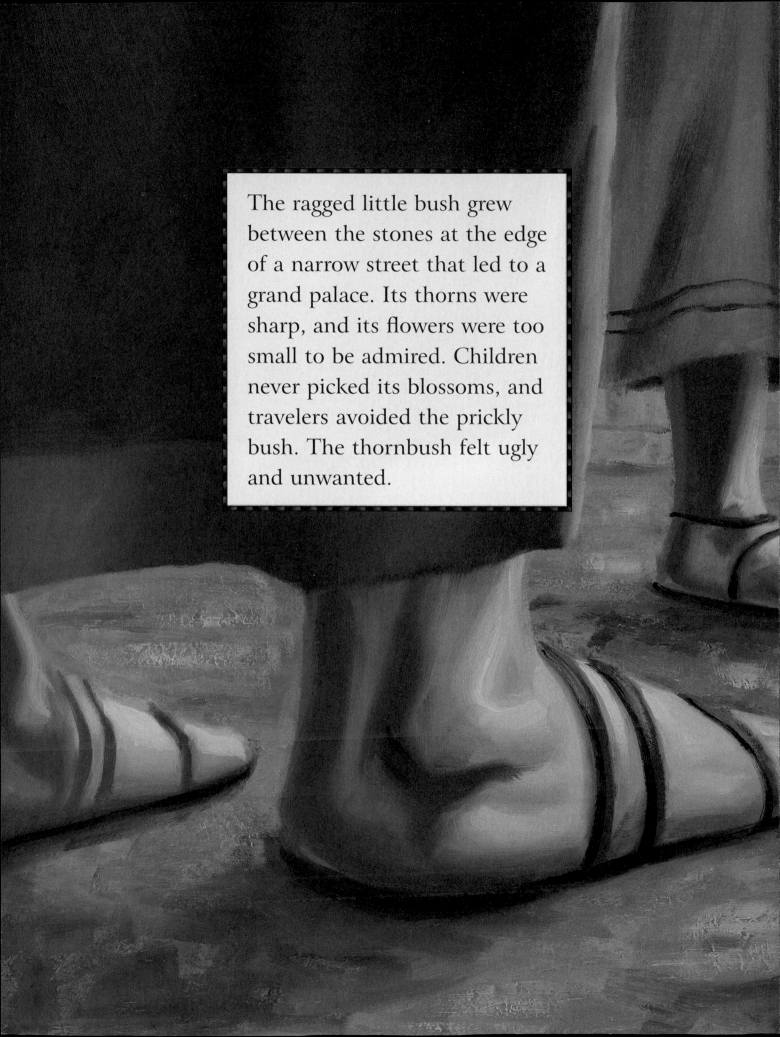

The ragged little bush grew between the stones at the edge of a narrow street that led to a grand palace. Its thorns were sharp, and its flowers were too small to be admired. Children never picked its blossoms, and travelers avoided the prickly bush. The thornbush felt ugly and unwanted.

A rooster crowed. Harsh voices stirred the thornbush from its sleep.

A crowd pushed a man through the quiet streets toward the palace. His hands were tied, but he showed no anger.

The man stopped in front of the little bush.

His gentle gaze made the bush feel warm and cared for. No one had ever shown such kindness to the thornbush. A moment later the shouting crowd forced the man to move on.

Out of the shadows came another man. As he passed, a silver coin fell to the ground. It rolled beneath the thornbush. The man knelt to pick it up. His face was sad, and he began to weep. His tears fell on the thornbush.

How I wish I could comfort him, thought the little bush, *but my thorns will only pierce him more.* The man stumbled off and did not return.

People began to gather outside the palace.

A soldier walked through the crowd toward the little thornbush.

The morning sunlight reflected off of the soldier's raised sword.

With a single swing of the sharp weapon, several branches fell from the little bush. The soldier gathered the cuttings and returned to the palace.

Why would anyone want my ugly thorns? the thornbush wondered.

The sun rose high in the morning sky. People began to shout as a man limped through the palace gates. "Behold your king, Jesus," laughed the soldiers, "who says he is the Son of God!"

"Crucify him!" yelled the angry mob.

The little bush shuddered. It was the man with the kind face. He was struggling to drag a heavy wooden cross over the rough stone street.

As the man reached the thornbush, he stumbled and fell to his knees. He turned a tired face toward the little bush.

Even though he will soon die on that cross, his eyes are filled with kindness, the little bush thought.

The thornbush recognized its own spiked branches weaved into a thorny crown upon the man's head.

A drop of blood fell from the man's forehead onto one of the bush's small yellow blooms. The stained flower fell to the ground.

It was a long, sad day. When all the people finally went home and the street was deserted, the thornbush bowed in sorrow. It was ashamed of the pain its thorns had caused the man with the cross.

For two days the thornbush refused to bloom. Morning dew fell like tears from its trembling branches.

The little bush bent low to examine the fallen flowers beneath it. Only one remained fresh—the flower stained by the blood of the man with the crown of thorns.

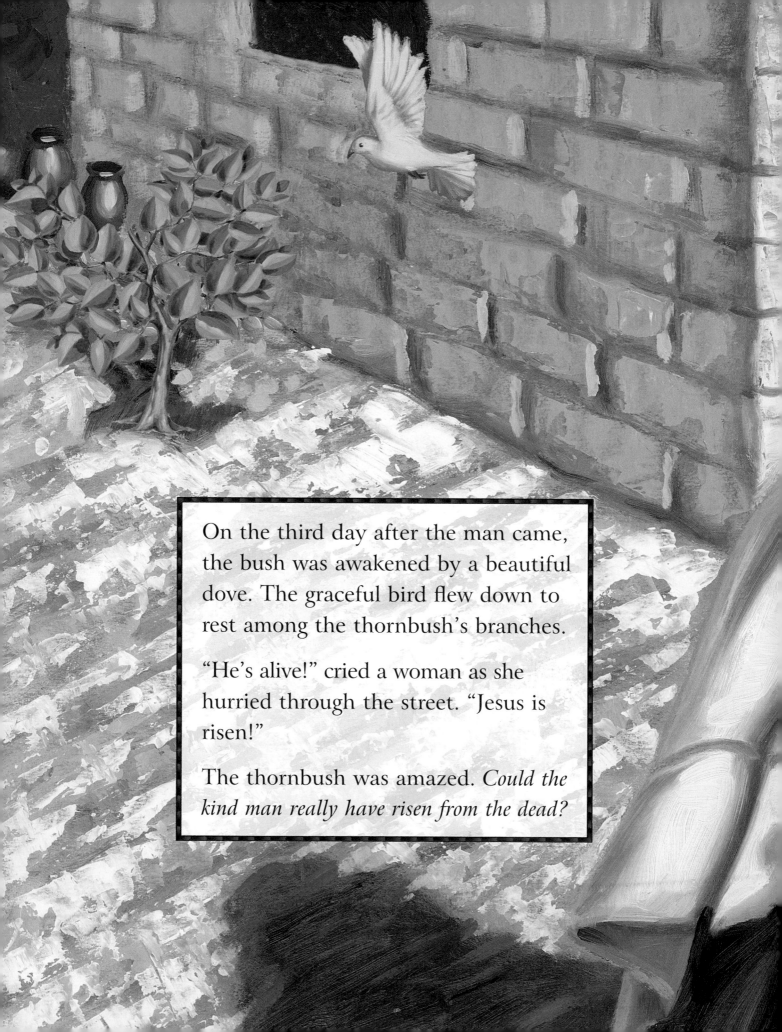

On the third day after the man came, the bush was awakened by a beautiful dove. The graceful bird flew down to rest among the thornbush's branches.

"He's alive!" cried a woman as she hurried through the street. "Jesus is risen!"

The thornbush was amazed. *Could the kind man really have risen from the dead?*

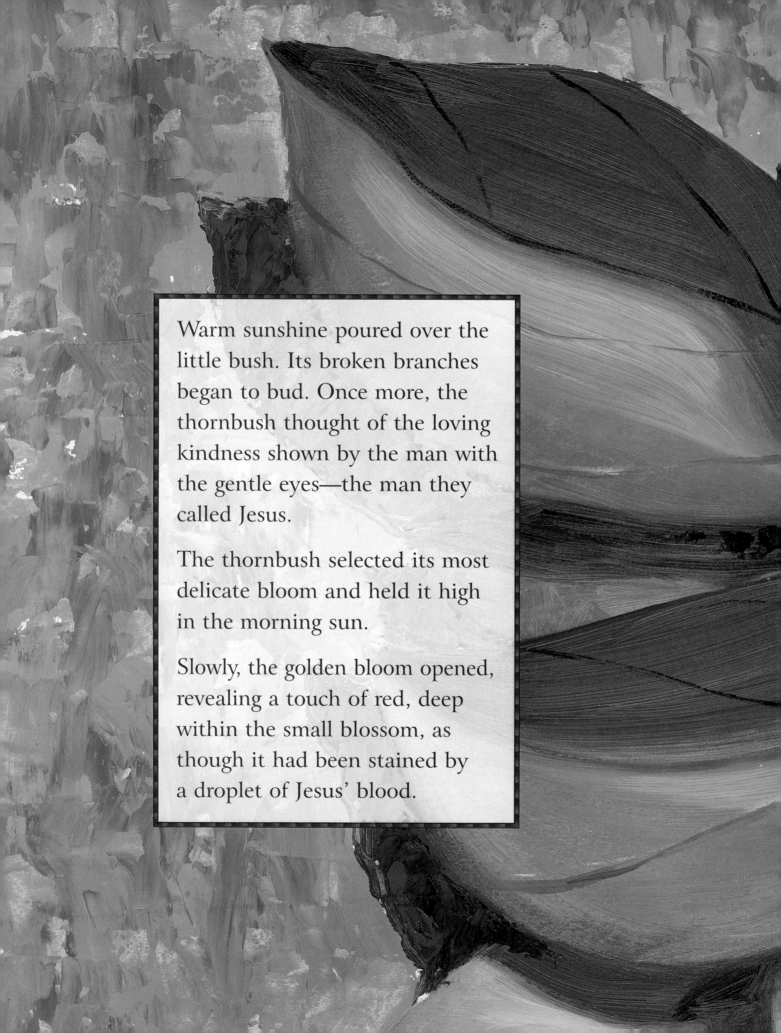

Warm sunshine poured over the little bush. Its broken branches began to bud. Once more, the thornbush thought of the loving kindness shown by the man with the gentle eyes—the man they called Jesus.

The thornbush selected its most delicate bloom and held it high in the morning sun.

Slowly, the golden bloom opened, revealing a touch of red, deep within the small blossom, as though it had been stained by a droplet of Jesus' blood.

The thornbush rejoiced! *The man, Jesus, had died but lived again! He truly is God's Son.* Jesus' only crown had been woven from the branches of the little thornbush. But that crown was greater than silver or gold.

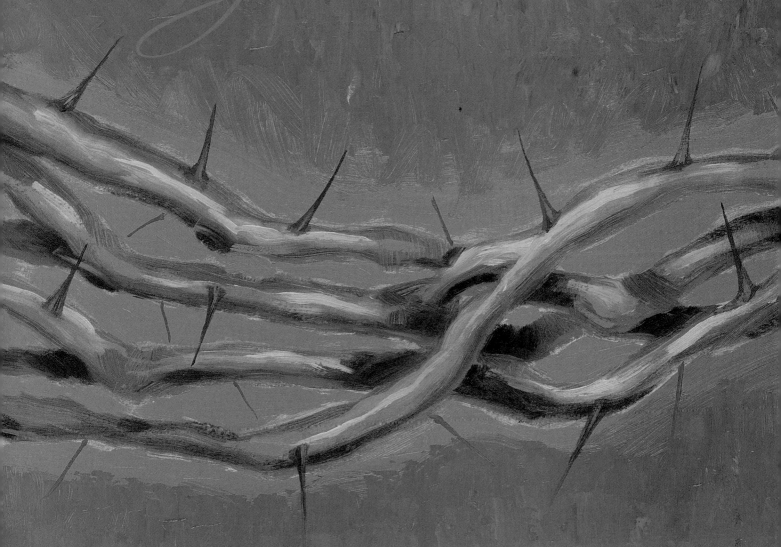

It was the crown of the

KING *of all* KINGS

JESUS

 **MICHAEL LAUGHLIN** is the father of two grown children, Emily and Christopher. He is a respected freelance writer and former magazine editor who has received numerous awards for writing and editing. Michael lives in Castle Rock, Colorado.

RICHARD STERGULZ is a freelance artist who, for the past thirteen years, has done both advertising and book illustration. He also shows his award-winning portraits and wildlife paintings in galleries. Richard resides in Oceanside, California, with his wife, Lisa.